POINTS OF

EARS
ATLAS
FORELOCK
TEMPLE
NOSE
PROJECTING CHEEK BONE
NASAL PEAK
NOSTRIL
MUZZLE
UPPER LIP
LOWER LIP
EYE
CHEEK
CHIN GROOVE
THROAT
POLL
AXIS
CREST
MANE
NECK
JUGULAR GROOVE
WIND PIPE
BASE OF NECK
WITHERS
SHOULDER
BREAST
FOREARM
KNEE
CANNON
FETLOCK JOINT
PASTERN
CORONET
WALL OF FOOT
ELBOW
TENDONS
POINT OF HIP
BACK
CHEST
BRISKET
CHESTNUT
ERGOT
POINT OF CROUP
LOINS
FLANK
RIBS
8 TRUE
10 FALSE
BELLY
SHEATH
STIFLE
SHIN
CHESTNUT
FETLOCK JOINT
PASTERN
CORONET
WALL OF FOOT
CROUP
HIP JOINT
THIGH
GASKIN
SHANK
DOCK
HAMSTRING
HOCK
TAIL
BUTTOCKS
POINT OF HOCK
FETLOCK
HEEL
POINT OF BUTTOCK

A Ladybird Book
Series 634

Here is a book which will help anyone who is learning to ride.

It gives helpful advice not only on such essential matters as how to insert a bit and put on a bridle and saddle, how to mount and dismount and which are the correct body, arm and leg positions, but also on trotting, cantering and jumping.

In addition, it offers useful information about understanding, grooming and caring for your pony.

Riding

by MARGARET HICKMAN

with illustrations by
JOHN BERRY

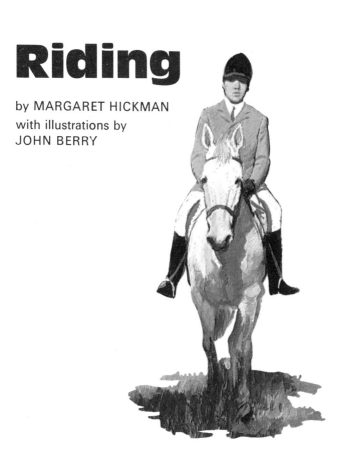

Ladybird Books Ltd Loughborough

Riding

Riding a pony is one of the most enjoyable ways of getting fresh air and exercise. It is not difficult to learn to ride. Try to go to a good riding school where you can be taught by a British Horse Society instructor.

Your first lessons are the most important. They will teach you how to sit properly in the saddle and the correct way to give instructions or 'aids' to your mount. Many people do not want to learn any more than this. They enjoy riding through the countryside and are not keen to jump or enter competitions. Other people are. They go on having lessons and become better and more experienced riders. It is all a matter of choice.

To all riders the pony is a good companion. He is a happy, intelligent animal with a mind of his own. If he is well treated and understood by his rider he will do his utmost to please.

Many disabled children are taught to ride. Sitting on a pony gives them a lot of enjoyment, and the balance needed for riding can help useless muscles to start working again.

4

0 7214 0357 3

Understanding the pony

A pony is not a machine. Like a human being, he has feelings, nerves and a brain. Always treat a pony with kindness and gentleness and he will work well for you. Speak to him quietly when you go up to him. Never make him jump by suddenly walking up behind and slapping him on the rump. Most important of all, do not be afraid of a pony. He can sense fear very easily and it will make him nervous. Never lose your temper.

If your pony will not do what you want the first time, ask him again, and keep asking him firmly until he obeys. Learn as much about ponies as you can. The better you understand them the better you will be able to ride them.

The pleasure with a pony comes not just from riding him, but from grooming him, talking to him and seeing to his needs. If ever you are lucky enough to own your own pony, you will soon find that he becomes as much a member of the family as a pet dog.

General information

The height of a pony is measured in hands. A hand is 4″ (102 mm). Stand the pony on level ground to measure him, and make him stand square. His height is the vertical distance from his withers to the ground.

There are many breeds of horse and pony. The most common for children to ride are the Mountain and Moorland ponies. Examples of these are the New Forest, Dartmoor, Exmoor and Welsh ponies.

Ponies vary in colour and each colour has a correct name. No pony is ever called white; it is always grey. A brown pony with black legs and a black mane and tail, is a bay. A very dark bay may, quite correctly, be called brown. A chestnut is a reddish or golden brown all over. There are very few black ponies; they may look black but are often a very dark bay. White with irregular black patches is called piebald. White with any other colour is skewbald. White fetlocks are socks. If the white hair extends over the knee or hock, it is a stocking. A small white mark between the eyes is called a star, but if the white runs down the length of the face it is a blaze.

Do not call the sides of a pony right and left. Looking from tail to head the right hand side is the offside and the left the nearside.

What to wear

The most important item of clothing for any rider is an approved hard hat. Wear this well forward, not perched on the back of your head, and always put the elastic under your chin. Then, if you fall off, your head will be protected. No one should ever ride a pony anywhere without wearing a hard hat.

The girl in the picture is properly dressed for riding. She has a hard hat, a shirt and tie, a riding jacket, gloves, breeches and long riding boots. She would be equally well-dressed in jodhpurs and short boots.

Riding clothes are expensive. If you are just starting to learn to ride, the only special clothes you need to buy are a hard hat and jodhpurs. Jodhpurs will stop the stirrup leathers from rubbing your legs and will not 'ride up' like jeans. Lace-up shoes which stay firmly on your feet are ideal for riding. Never wear slip-on shoes or Wellingtons, as they can catch in the stirrup irons. Leather or string gloves should always be worn to stop the reins from slipping through your hands.

Always look neat and tidy when you go riding and then, even if you have not got all the right clothes, you will look a proficient rider.

Grooming

All ponies must be groomed before they are ridden. If you put a saddle on a dirty pony he can get a sore back from the rubbing of dirt between the leather and his skin.

Tie up the pony with a slip-knot in his halter so that if he pulls back, the knot can still be undone. Use a dandy brush first to get the mud off his coat. This brush has stiff bristles and a lot of dust and grease will rise to the surface of his coat when using it. To get rid of this, brush the pony with a soft body brush, using circular strokes to clean the coat and massage the skin.

After every few strokes, run the bristles over the teeth of a curry comb to free them of dirt. Tap the side of the curry comb on the floor to get rid of the grease. Finish with a straw wisp and a stable rubber or cloth to leave a shine on his coat. Use a dandy brush on his mane and tail. The mane comb is used to 'pull' or thin out the hairs.

Pick out his feet with the hoof pick. Wipe his nostrils and eyes with a damp cloth and clean under his tail with a second damp cloth.

If the pony is being groomed for a special occasion, you may wash his tail and then put on a tail bandage to keep the hairs smooth. Roll a tail bandage with the tapes on the inside and put it on firmly from the top to the bottom of the dock.

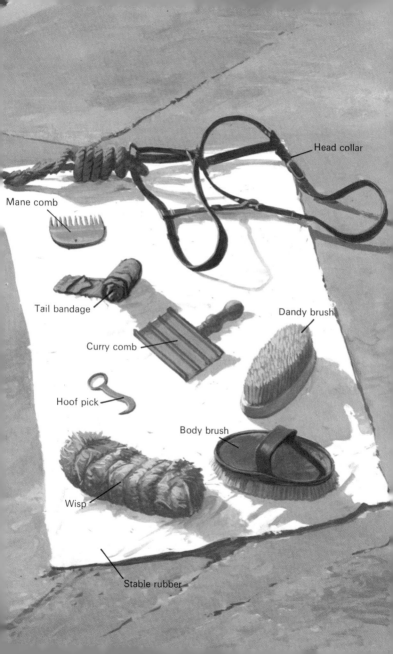

Head collar

Mane comb

Tail bandage

Dandy brush

Curry comb

Hoof pick

Body brush

Wisp

Stable rubber

Hooves

There is an old saying, 'No foot, no horse!'

A rider *must* take care of the pony's feet. They should be examined every day. To pick up a pony's hoof, stand by his side facing his tail and run your nearest hand down the back of his leg until you reach the fetlock joint. A gentle pull upwards will usually make the pony lift his hoof.

Slide your hand round the hoof to support it while it is off the ground. Underneath you will see a triangular, spongy area called the frog. Clean out the pony's hooves every day with a hoof pick. This has a blunted end. Never use anything sharp. Scrape all the dirt out of the hoof and from the groove round the frog. Always work downwards away from the frog and the bulb of the heel.

If any stones are left in the pony's hooves he may go lame. While you are holding up his hoof, check that his shoe is still in good condition. If any of the nails are sticking out, or the shoe is worn thin, or the whole shoe is loose, the blacksmith should be called at once.

The blacksmith

A pony wears iron shoes on his feet to protect them from the hard ground. The shoes are put on by a black-smith and will last about two months unless the pony is ridden on the roads every day. Every rider should know something about shoeing.

When the pony is shod, the blacksmith takes off the old shoes and cuts back the hoof to a neat shape. Then he heats each new shoe in a furnace before holding it in place on the pony's foot so that it burns to a snug fit. This does not hurt the pony at all. The shoe has a groove on the side nearest the ground and the black-smith nails the shoe to the hoof along this groove. He puts more nails along the outside than the inside because the shoe is longer on the outside.

The blacksmith must be very careful when he puts the nails in. They must go only in the thin horn wall of the hoof. Inside this wall is flesh. The nails go in at an angle and, where they come out through the horn, the blacksmith cuts them off short, turns the ends over and files the hoof smooth.

The nail ends are called clenches, and when these begin to rise it shows that the shoes are wearing out. At the front of each shoe there is a raised piece of metal which fits up into the hoof. This is a clip.

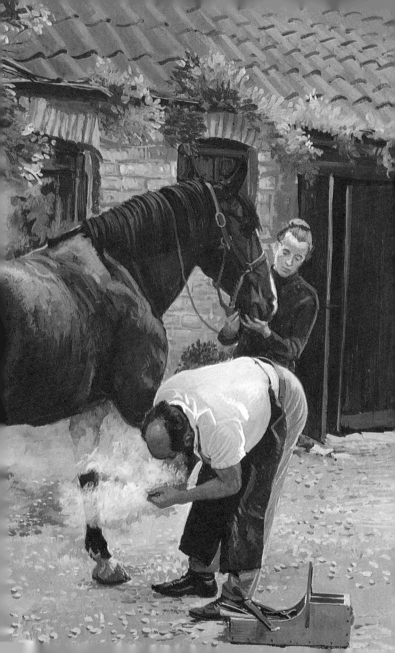

Putting on a bridle

Check that none of the bridle straps is twisted. The throat lash and the noseband must be unfastened.

Put the reins round the pony's neck and take off his halter. Hold the headpiece of the bridle in your right hand. Lay the bit on the palm of your left hand. Do not bang the bit against the pony's teeth to make him open his mouth. Tuck your fingers into the corners of his lips where he has no teeth and push his jaws apart. As you lift the bit into his mouth, pull the rest of the bridle up towards the top of his head. Gently draw his ears and forelock under the headpiece.

Fasten the throat lash so that four fingers can be placed between the strap and his cheek. Fasten the noseband so that two fingers can be slipped between the strap and his nose. The noseband itself should lie two fingers below the cheekbone. Check that the bit is just wrinkling the corners of his mouth. It is important to see that your pony is comfortable in his bridle. If anything is too tight or too loose, or the straps are not fastened down neatly, it will worry him and he will not give his full attention to his work.

See endpaper for details of a snaffle bridle.

Bits

There are many different kinds of bit but they are nearly all variations of two common types. The snaffle is the most usual bit to see on a pony. The bar of the bit can be smooth or twisted and of different thicknesses. Some have loose rings and others have fixed rings. A snaffle has one rein attached to each ring. The thinner the bar of the bit, the more severe it is, and a bar with a twist is stronger than one without.

A pelham is used on a pony that pulls or has a hard mouth. The pelham has no joint in the middle of the bit but has a straight bar at each end. Two reins attach to the two rings on each bar. A chain called a curb chain runs from one end of the bit to the other and lies in the groove behind the pony's chin. The curb chain must always be unhooked before you put on the bridle, and twisted until it lies flat before being done up. The lower rein on the pelham tips the bit in the pony's mouth so the curb chain tightens behind his jaw. If only the top rein is tightened the curb chain stays loose.

A kimblewick is often used on a pony. This is exactly like an ordinary pelham except that it has only one rein which always tightens the curb chain.

A double bridle is used for advanced riding. The pony has both a snaffle and a pelham type bit in his mouth at the same time when he wears a double bridle.

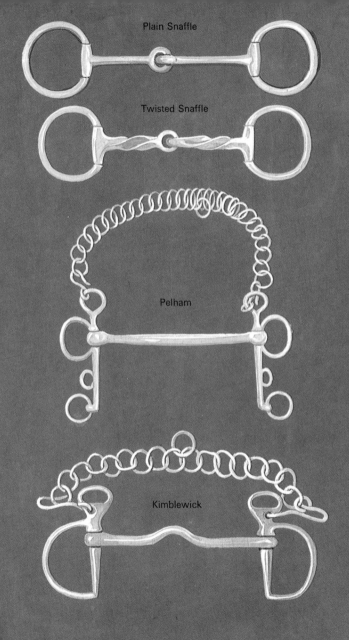

Plain Snaffle

Twisted Snaffle

Pelham

Kimblewick

Putting on a saddle

Make sure that the stirrup irons are run up the leathers and that the girths are laid across the seat of the saddle. Put the saddle on from the near side. Lift it up on your left arm. Place it down gently on the pony's back so the pommel is well over the withers. Then, with a hand on the pommel and cantle, slide the saddle back until it lies comfortably in the hollow of his back.

Go round to the offside and take down the girths. Make sure they hang straight. If you have two girths, lay the front girth under the back girth. Fasten the girths on the near side. Fold back the saddle flap to get at the girth straps. Reach under the pony for the girth and buckle the two straps securely. There are three straps for the two buckles. Use the first and last, or the first two, as the last two are attached to the same piece of webbing in the construction of the saddle. Run your fingers under the girths to make sure no skin is pinched.

Some ponies wear a sheepskin numnah or a thick saddle cloth under their saddles. If they do, push it up into the groove under the saddle so that air can get to the pony's back when the saddle is on and there is no pressure on his spine.

See endpaper for details of a saddle.

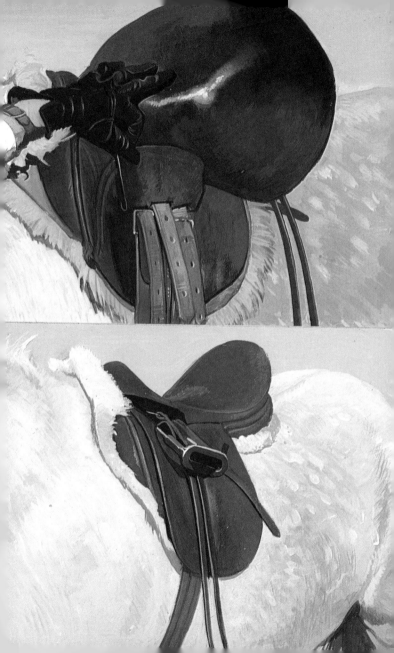

Extra saddlery

Most ponies wear just a saddle and a bridle but there are some extra pieces of harness, or tack, that you will meet.

Martingales are used to keep a pony's head in the correct position. There are standing and running martingales. Both go between the front legs and are attached to the girth. They are held in place by a neck strap and a rubber stop. A standing martingale is a single piece of leather attached to the noseband. It stops the pony looking at the sky or star gazing. A running martingale has two straps, each ending with a ring which runs on the rein. When you pull on the reins, the martingale holds them down and keeps the pony's nose in. Always put rubber stops on the reins, on the bit side of the martingale rings, to stop them catching on the bit.

A drop noseband is a low noseband lying just above the nostrils. It runs outside and below the rings of the bit and fastens in the chin groove. A drop noseband stops a pony opening his mouth. Take care that the drop noseband is not put on too low or too tight or it will interfere with the pony's breathing.

Girths can be leather, webbing, nylon or string. The picture shows a nylon or string girth.

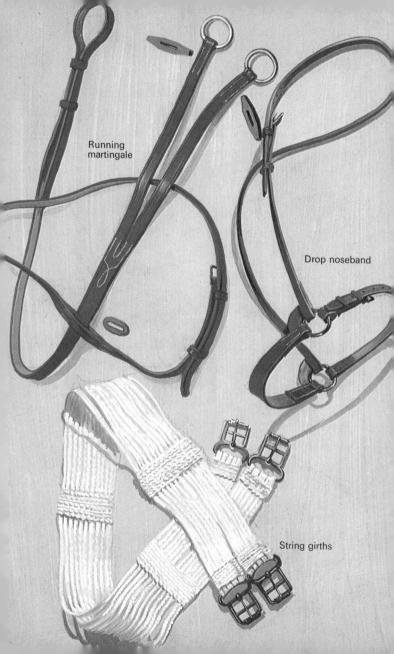

Running martingale

Drop noseband

String girths

Mounting

Check that your pony's girths are tight. Stand the pony on level ground. Mount from the near side, facing the tail. Hold both reins in your left hand, with the loose ends hanging down the far side of the pony's neck. Rest this hand on the pommel. Keep the reins firm, but not tight, to stop the pony walking away. Hold the stirrup leather in your right hand and turn the iron towards you ready for your left foot. With your left foot in the stirrup, and your right hand on the waist of the saddle, move round to face the saddle. Make sure you do not dig the pony in the ribs with your left foot.

With a slight hop, spring up to bring the right foot level with the left, steadying yourself with your right hand on the back of the saddle. Then swing your right leg over the back of the saddle and sit down gently. Mounting should be a smooth movement, never a scramble up the side of the pony. Slip your other foot into the stirrup iron. Pick your reins up in both hands. Do not ask the pony to move until you are comfortable.

If a pony will not stand still to be mounted, have the left rein a little tighter than the right so that he circles towards you and can still be mounted easily.

Hand position

The reins are not for helping you to keep your balance, like the handlebars of a bicycle. You must keep only the lightest hold on the pony's mouth through the reins. Avoid tugging or jerking at them. Hold them in both hands.

Pick up the reins, one in each hand, with your thumbs towards you and your knuckles uppermost. Then turn your hands over so that your finger nails face one another and your thumbs are uppermost. The thumb of your right hand must point towards the pony's left ear and your left thumb towards the right ear.

Let the reins run through your palms and between your little and third fingers. Keep your wrists relaxed and your hands together. Your arms, hands or wrists must not be stiff. Keep your hands down near the pommel of the saddle but not resting on it. Your elbows must stay close to your sides. Hold the reins just tight enough to be able to 'feel' the pony's mouth. As he moves at different paces you must keep the same 'feel'.

If you are carrying a stick, hold it in your left hand together with the left rein. Do not let it stick out sideways but rest it across your thigh.

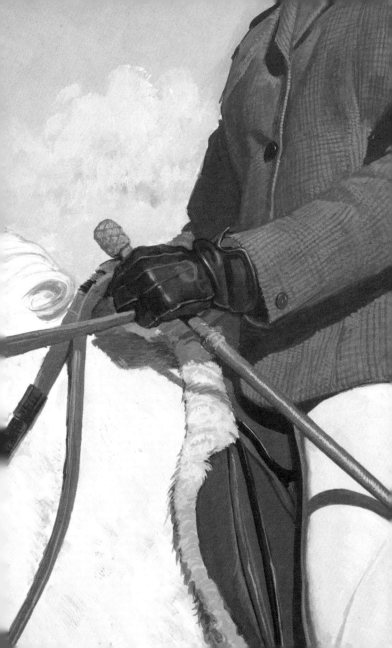

Leg position

After mounting, adjust the length of your stirrups. Seated without your legs in the stirrups, the bottoms of the irons should be level with your ankle bones.

Keep your legs close to the pony's sides. A straight line drawn down your body to the ground should pass through your ear, shoulder, hip and heel. Put the ball of your foot on the stirrup iron. Push your weight down into your heels.

To get the correct leg position, feel your two seat bones pressing on the saddle. Turn your thighs inwards so that the whole of the inside of your leg—thigh, knee and calf—is close against the pony's side. Do not grip tightly with your knees or calves because this will make you stiff and tense. Just keep a close, relaxed contact down the whole length of each leg. Do not grip with your heels or your legs will gradually work back and up. Keep your feet parallel to the pony's sides.

When you want your pony to alter his pace, just squeeze his sides with your calves. If he does not obey, increase the pressure of your legs and just touch his sides with your heels as an instruction to go faster. Never give him a hefty kick in the ribs.

General position and the aids

Sit straight on your pony and keep your head up to see where you are going. Never lean back or you may lose your balance and jerk the pony's mouth. Keep your hands down, your elbows in and your toes up.

The instructions to a pony to change his pace or direction are called aids. You never shake the reins and call 'gee up' to make a pony move. The aids to walk and trot in a straight line are the same. Keep a firm, not a tight hold on the pony's mouth through the reins and squeeze with your legs until the pony responds. As soon as he does what you ask, stop using the aid. Use both legs evenly and make sure the right and left rein are the same length. To stop the pony, pull gently on the reins and just feel his sides with your legs to keep him balanced. Do not lean back. The aid to canter is included in the section on the canter.

To turn to the right or left, feel the rein on the side that you want to turn to and loosen the other rein to allow the turn. Give a little pressure on the pony's side with the outside leg to prevent him swinging his quarters out. Squeeze with the inside leg to keep the pony moving with energy (impulsion). This is the most important leg.

Head and
chin up

Back
straight

Elbows in

Hands low

Contact
with
whole
leg

First lessons

The first time you mount a pony it will probably feel very strange. You will hold onto the mane or the front of the saddle to keep your balance and feel that the ground is a very long way away. The most important thing is to build up confidence in yourself and your pony. With confidence comes balance. Riding is mainly balance. You must sit firmly in the saddle but never stiffly. As the pony moves you must not try to sit rigidly in the correct position. Go with the pony. Feel that you are moving with him. As soon as you do this you will begin to feel perfectly safe and you will balance naturally on his back. To get this confidence and to learn balance you will probably spend your first few lessons on a leading rein. This is a long rein for the instructor to hold, which is attached to both sides of the bit. You do not need to worry then about the pony running away or going in the wrong direction. All your concentration will be on keeping a good position and getting used to the feel of your pony.

Trotting

Trotting is probably the most difficult riding pace. The trot is the one pace where your seat leaves the saddle. You go up and down with a steady rhythm in time with the pony's stride. This is called rising to the trot. It is a knack which can come only with practice.

To trot, you lift your seat off the saddle, taking the weight of your body on your knees, calves and the ball of your foot in the stirrup iron. Then come gently back into the saddle. Never come down with a bang. The rise and fall must be controlled.

The trot itself feels bumpy, and it is up to you to catch the bumps and rise from the saddle away from them. Count to yourself, one, two, one, two, in time with the pony's stride and rise and fall to the count. Trotting is a rhythm that you will not get into unless you relax and go with the pony. Keep your weight forward so you do not lose your balance. Keep your hands low and look straight ahead.

Cantering

The canter is a pleasant, smooth pace. Just sit down in the saddle and go with the pony. Do not sit hard down in the saddle. Sway backwards and forwards very slightly from the hips, keeping time with the pony. In the canter the pony strikes out with one foreleg always in front of the other. If the near foreleg is the leading one, the pony is said to be on the left leg, if the off foreleg is leading, it is on the right leg. If you are cantering in a circle, the inside foreleg must always lead.

A pony can be made to canter on whichever leg you wish. To canter with the off foreleg leading, the aid is to feel the right rein and move your left leg back behind the girth to squeeze the pony's side. Never look down or lean over sideways to see if he is leading on the correct leg. Look at his shoulders. You will see one moving further forward than the other and that is the shoulder of the leading leg.

Jumping

You will not learn to jump until you can walk, trot and canter properly. Jumping is not difficult. To jump a pony, do not alter the position of your legs at all. Ask the pony to move towards the jump at a steady pace. When he reaches the jump, increase the pressure of your legs against his sides to make him take off. Do not kick him in the ribs. As he rises, lean your body forward and slide your hands up his neck. This will stop you from getting 'left behind', which means being thrown off balance so that you lean back and jerk on the bit. Leaning forward also takes the weight off the pony's back as he jumps. Jumping must be a smooth action for both pony and rider. As the pony lands he will canter on and you must sit up straight again and bring your hands back to their normal position. Always jump holding the reins in both hands. Never look down. Keep your head up and look between the pony's ears so that you can see where you are going.

Start your jumping lessons over thick poles laid flat on the ground about $4\frac{1}{2}$ feet (1.4 metres) apart. Trot your pony over these until you feel quite safe, then canter over the same poles. When you start jumping small fences, make sure they are solidly built so that the pony does not drop his feet through them. A pole laid on the ground a little distance in front of the fence will make the pony take off properly and give you a smooth and comfortable jump.

Exercises

Everyone who is learning to ride should do exercises on the pony. Exercises to move your arms and legs and body help you to get a good balance. You will not always ride quiet ponies and the better the pony the quicker and more sudden are his movements. Exercises teach you to keep your basic riding position whilst some other parts of you are doing something else. Exercises also strengthen your riding muscles and make you fitter. You will get more confidence by moving about on a pony and finding that you do not fall off.

The girl in the picture is touching her toes without moving her legs from their correct position against the pony's sides. There are many other exercises. Sit up straight with your arms held out at shoulder level and swing round as far as possible in the direction of the pony's tail, without moving your legs. Cross your stirrups over the front of the saddle and get someone to lead the pony at a walk and trot, while you keep your correct position without the help of stirrups.

A happy pony

A pony is an intelligent animal who can get very bored by doing the same thing over and over again. Most ponies enjoy their work but they need variety. They are like human beings. You may like to walk in the park but you would soon get bored if you went the same way every day. Take your pony different rides so that he is interested in where he is going. Do not turn left at a particular cross roads every time or he may object if one day you decide to turn right.

Keep off the main roads as much as possible. If there is a grass verge, and it is not part of someone's garden, ride your pony on that. It is softer for his feet than tarmac. If the verge is wide enough and safe, you may be able to canter and perhaps jump a few little ditches.

Look for bridle paths and cross-country tracks where you are allowed to ride.

Keep your pony wondering where he is going and then he will stride out with his ears pricked and a happy look in his eyes. Nothing is more uninteresting than riding a bored pony.

Riding in company

You do not have to ride alone. Ponies enjoy company. When you do ride with other ponies, take care not to ride too close to the pony ahead. He may kick out. Leave a pony's length between you and the pony in front.

There are a number of clubs and pony gatherings that you can attend. The Pony Club is a good way to meet other riders. There are branches all over England. Pony Club members can go to a summer camp with their ponies, take tests to prove how good their horsemanship is and may even be lucky enough to get into a team to compete for the Prince Philip Cup in mounted games. Riding clubs also provide a way to ride in competitions and to learn more about ponies. All through the summer there are horse shows, not only for jumping but for gymkhana events and best rider classes.

Dressage is for riders who enjoy making their ponies so obedient that they will alter their pace and direction at special points marked in a small arena.

Event riding combines dressage with show jumping and cross-country jumping.

Some people like to hunt, but they must be good enough riders to take their ponies across country, jumping the hedges and ditches that divide the fields.

Dismounting

Always dismount on the left or near side. Make the pony stand still. Take your feet out of both stirrups. Put the reins in your left hand, keeping a 'feel' on the pony's mouth so that he does not walk off. Lean forward, steadying yourself with your hands on the pommel. Swing your right leg clear of the back of the saddle, twisting your body so that you slide down the side of the pony. Keep your balance with your hands on the pommel and cantle of the saddle and land quietly on both feet.

If you have dismounted because it is the end of the ride, loop the reins over your arm and run both stirrups up to the top of their leathers. Always loosen the girths if the pony is to stand for any length of time with his saddle on. Slide the reins over the pony's head ready to lead him into his stable.

Lead a pony from the near side. Hold both reins together. Keep your right hand close under his chin and take the slack of the reins in your left. When you lead a pony round a corner always push him away from you so that he cannot turn very sharply and knock you over.

The end of the ride

Walk your pony the last half mile of his ride to try and bring him home cool and unexcited. If he has been sweating and is still warm, loosen his girths and lead him round until he is dry. Take off his saddle and bridle and put on his halter. Brush him over to remove any sweat marks and mud. Clean out his feet to make sure no stones have got caught in his frogs or under his shoes.

If your pony lives in a field, never turn him out until you are certain that he is happy and comfortable. Lead him into the field and turn him round to face the gate before you take off his halter. Then, if he kicks up his heels as he moves away, you will not get hurt.

Always give your pony a titbit before you leave him in the field or the stable. Ponies love carrots and apples. They also like sugar, but too much sugar is bad for their teeth. Hold the titbit flat on the palm of your hand with your fingers close together so that the pony can take his reward without taking your fingers as well.

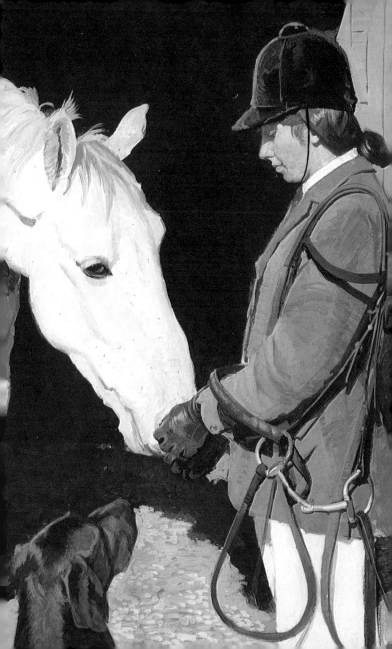

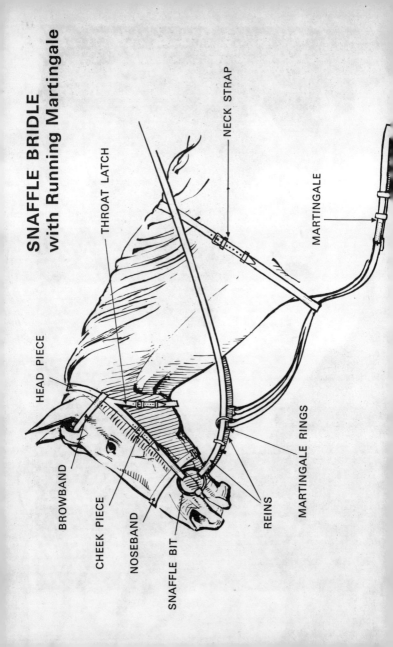

SNAFFLE BRIDLE
with Running Martingale

NECK STRAP

THROAT LATCH

MARTINGALE

HEAD PIECE

BROWBAND

CHEEK PIECE

NOSEBAND

SNAFFLE BIT

REINS

MARTINGALE RINGS